25p

The
Tiara
Club

KU-185-428

For Princess Megan B, and all the other
princesses at Park Hill School, Wednesbury
VF

www.tiaraclub.co.uk

First published in 2007 by Orchard Books

ORCHARD BOOKS
338 Euston Road, London NW1 3BH
Orchard Books Australia
Level 17/207 Kent St, Sydney NSW 2000

A Paperback Original

A CIP catalogue record for this book is availablee
from the British Library.

ISBN 978 1 84616 570 2

1 3 5 7 9 10 8 6 4 2

Printed and bound in Denmark by Nørhaven Paperback A/S

Orchard Books is a division of Hachette Children's Books
www.orchardbooks.co.uk

The Tiara Club

Princess Megan

and the **Magical Tiara**

By Vivian French

ORCHARD BOOKS

The Royal Palace Academy
for the Preparation of Perfect Princesses

(Known to our students as "*The Princess Academy*")

OUR SCHOOL MOTTO:
*A Perfect Princess always thinks of others
before herself, and is kind, caring and truthful.*

Silver Towers offers a complete education for
Tiara Club princesses with emphasis on selected
outings. The curriculum includes:

Fans and Curtseys	*Problem Prime Ministers*
A visit to Witch Windlespin	*A visit to the Museum of Royal Life*
(Royal herbalist, healer and maker of magic potions)	*(Students will be well protected from the Poisoned Apple)*

Our headteacher, Queen Samantha Joy, is present
at all times, and students are well looked after
by the school Fairy Godmother, Fairy Angora.

Our resident staff and visiting experts include:

LADY ALBINA MacSPLINTER *(School Secretary)*	QUEEN MOTHER MATILDA *(Etiquette, Posture and Poise)*
CROWN PRINCE DANDINO *(School Excursions)*	FAIRY G *(Head Fairy Godmother)*

We award tiara points to encourage our Tiara Club princesses towards the next level. All princesses who win enough points at Silver Towers will attend the Silver Ball, where they will be presented with their Silver Sashes.

Silver Sash Tiara Club princesses are invited to return to Ruby Mansions, our exclusive residence for Perfect Princesses, where they may continue their education at a higher level.

PLEASE NOTE:
Princesses are expected to arrive at the Academy with a *minimum* of:

TWENTY BALLGOWNS
(with all necessary hoops, petticoats, etc)

TWELVE DAY DRESSES

SEVEN GOWNS
suitable for garden parties, and other special day occasions

TWELVE TIARAS

DANCING SHOES
five pairs

VELVET SLIPPERS
three pairs

RIDING BOOTS
two pairs

Cloaks, muffs, stoles, gloves and other essential accessories as required

Chapter One

Hi! I'm Princess Megan, and I'm SO pleased to meet you.

Are you a Perfect Princess? I'm not – although I do try. But when my parents told me they were sending me to the Princess Academy, I wasn't at ALL perfect. I wasn't calm, or graceful, or even polite. I absolutely shrieked with joy, and danced round and round the room. I'd been dying to go away to school for AGES, but my parents had always said no before. Grandmother taught me at home, and of course I loved her, but I was longing to make friends with other princesses. I'd read LOADS of books about boarding schools, and I just knew I'd have a BRILLIANT time.

"What's it like? Where is it? Can I stay for ever and ever?" I couldn't get my questions out fast enough.

My mother sighed. "Megan dear, DO try and behave. It's the Royal Palace Academy for the Preparation of Perfect Princesses,

8

and you'll be joining the princesses in Silver Towers."

"When am I going? Oh – will I need masses of new clothes?" I looked hopefully at my father.

He glanced at my mother. "I understand you'll need a new ballgown. Now, run upstairs. Your grandmother wants to see you."

I fairly flew up to my rooms. Grandmother was waiting for me, and I flung myself at her.

"Guess what, darling Gran! I'm going to school!'

"About time too, poppet," she said. "And I want you to be the prettiest princess at the Academy, so I thought you should have this." She handed me a parcel wrapped in pink tissue paper.

"Thank you!" I said, and I ripped off the paper – and I was DAZZLED! I was holding the most GORGEOUS sparkly tiara. It was SO lovely, it took my breath away. "Thank you SOOOO much!" I gave Gran a huge hug. "It's the most wonderful tiara I've ever seen. It looks totally magical!"

Grandmother gave me a funny little sideways look. "Maybe it is," she said. "You'll certainly find it knows who it belongs to. But now we must talk about your new ballgown!"

I don't think I've ever been so happy in my entire life!

Chapter Two

I kept begging the coachman to go faster all the way to the Princess Academy. I just couldn't WAIT to meet masses of new friends, and to wear my amazing tiara and my utterly GORGEOUS new satin ball gown with puff sleeves and lacy overskirts. When the coach finally bowled up to Silver Towers' front door I practically fell out, I was in such a hurry.

There were two girls waiting for me at the front door, and I rushed towards them. They were twins, and really pretty – but they had the most stuck-up expressions you could imagine. When I said "Hello!" they didn't even smile.

"Oh dear," said the first one as she stared at me. "YOU must be Princess Megan. Have you been to a Princess Academy before?"

"No," I said. "My grandmother's always taught me my lessons."

The second twin burst out laughing. "Your GRANDMOTHER?" she

sneered. "Oh goodness me. Poor little Megan will have a LOT to learn, won't she, Diamonde?"

Diamonde sniggered. "I'll say."
She looked at my clothes, and it was
obvious she didn't think much
of them. "Have you got any pretty
dresses? There's a Tiara Ball tonight,
and we'll all be wearing the most
fabulous ballgowns and tiaras.
Won't we, Gruella?"

Gruella tossed her hair back.
"That's right. And WE'LL be the
best-dressed princesses there."

"Oh," I said. I couldn't think of
anything else to say.

Diamonde rolled her eyes at
Gruella. "I suppose we'd better take
Megan up to Silver Rose Room."

"I suppose we had." Gruella

sighed loudly. And she and
Diamonde zoomed off, while
I scuttled behind them. We seemed
to go through an absolute maze of
stairs and corridors, but at last
Gruella threw open a door.

"Here you are. You'd better go in and wait for the others." She pushed me inside, and flounced away.

A second later Diamonde put her head back round the door.

"It's all right," she whispered. "Gruella and I won't tell. You needn't worry."

I stared at her in amazement. "Worry about what?"

Diamonde made her eyes very big and wide. "Why, that you've never been to school before. EVERYBODY else has – except for the servants, of course. I don't know HOW you were allowed to come here, actually. Just don't EVER tell anyone, or DREADFUL things will happen to you!" And then she was gone.

Chapter Three

I stood in the middle of the dormitory, my stomach full of flutters. Why was it so terrible that I'd never been to school before? I almost wished I could go home. I was a little bit cheered up, though, because the dormitory was just as lovely as I'd imagined. It had soft pink walls, and the beds had the prettiest red velvet cushions on them. There were seven beds, but the seventh had obviously been brought in as an extra, because it was tucked against the wall at the end.

"Oh no!" I thought. "What if the other princesses are like those horrid twins, and they don't want me to share with them?" But I didn't have time to worry because the door burst open, and in rushed a girl with the loveliest smile.

"Are you Princess Megan?" she gasped. "I'm Alice, and I'm SO sorry we weren't here when you arrived – you must think we're just HORRIBLE!"

Before I could answer, five more princesses came hurrying in, and the tallest made me the most perfect curtsey. "I'm Princess Sophia. I'm VERY pleased to meet you."

Then Katie, Charlotte, Daisy and Emily introduced themselves and curtsied too, and I curtsied back – but I wasn't nearly as good as they were. I wobbled, and that made Charlotte giggle.

"I once fell over right in front of

our headteacher," she told me. "I felt TERRIBLE!" She sat down on the bed next to me. "Has your luggage arrived yet?"

"I'm not sure," I said, but at that very moment two pages came marching in with my trunk.

"For Princess Megan," they said, and marched away again.

"Have you got a dress for the Tiara Ball?" Emily asked as I began to unpack. "It's tonight, and there's going to be a Tiara Parade as well!"

I pulled out my beautiful new satin dress. "Do you think this is all right?"

"OOOOOOOOH!" My six new friends oohed and aaahed.

"It's absolutely GORGEOUS!" Katie breathed. "Have you got a tiara to match?"

"Yes," I said, and I pulled out my magical tiara.

"WOW!" Charlotte's eyes were

huge. "I've NEVER seen such sparkly diamonds!"

"We'll be very proud to know you," Daisy said shyly. "You'll look wonderful."

"Thank you," I said, and the flutters in my stomach disappeared completely. "What are you going to wear?"

Katie jumped up from where she was sitting. "We've got an least an hour before tea. Let's have a dress rehearsal!"

Chapter Four

By the time we were dressed in our ballgowns I felt as if I'd known the others for AGES. We giggled together, and helped each other with our sashes and bows, and it was SUCH fun. We were having a mini parade round the room when there was a knock on the door, and Diamonde came in with her nose in the air.

"Queen Samantha Joy told me to tell you tea's early tonight, so we have time to get ready for the ball," she began, and then she stopped dead. She was staring and STARING at my tiara.

"There's one other thing," she went on slowly, "a private message for Megan. Come outside, Megan, and I'll tell you."

"Yes," I said. "Of course—" but as soon as I was out of the door Diamonde dragged me down the empty corridor.

"You remember Gruella and I said we wouldn't tell anyone you hadn't ever been to school?" she hissed in my ear.

"Yes," I said.

"Well, we MIGHT be about to change our minds." She gave me a spiteful glare. I didn't know what to say, so I said nothing.

"If we DO tell, you'll be taken away from Silver Rose Room," Diamonde went on. "Did you know that? You'll be sent to the reception class – or they might even send you home!"

A lump came into my throat. I SO wanted to stay in Silver Rose Room. "Please don't tell," I whispered. "PLEASE!"

"Well..." Diamonde hesitated. "I promise we won't tell if—" she looked greedily at my beautiful diamond tiara – "IF you let me wear your tiara this evening!"

I gulped, and my stomach was FULL of flutters. "I...all right.

You can wear it."

Diamonde grinned a triumphant grin.

"I'll see you outside the ballroom," she said. "Make sure you're there early!"

"I will," I promised miserably.

I trailed back to Silver Rose Room, and tried to pretend nothing had happened as I took off my dress. The others were much too

polite to ask me what Diamonde had said, but they could see something was wrong, and they were SO sweet. They kept telling me

how glad they were I'd come to Silver Towers, and it should have made me feel LOADS better – but it didn't. I felt totally sick. Was Diamonde going to tell? Or was she just going to go on and ON making me do things I didn't want to do?

Chapter Five

I couldn't eat much tea, even though Alice tried her best to cheer me up. Charlotte told me funny stories, and Emily and Daisy kept looking at me anxiously. Katie and Sophia did too, but it made everything worse. They were the nicest friends I'd ever had, and I couldn't bear the thought of being sent away from them.

And I SO didn't want to lend Diamonde my tiara. It was all a terrible mix-up, and I didn't know WHAT to do.

On the way back up to Silver Rose Room Katie tucked her arm through mine.

"Honestly," she said, "I'm not trying to interfere, but do remember Perfect Princesses sometimes have to stick up for themselves. Diamonde and Gruella are absolutely horrible—"

"KATIE!" Sophia sounded really shocked. *"Perfect princesses do NOT speak ill of others.* It's one of the most important rules!"

Katie winked at me. "No, they shouldn't, but they can't help THINKING it!"

"Thank you SO much," I said, and I meant it. And as I began to get ready for the Tiara Ball, I went on thinking about what Katie had said. Maybe I should stick up for myself...but it was a VERY scary thought.

I was ready first. My dress looked lovely, but I didn't put my tiara on. Emily asked if I wanted any help.

"It's OK, thank you," I said. "I...I'm going to put it on when I get downstairs."

I wanted to go on my own to meet Diamonde, but I didn't know the way, so I had to wait for the others. They looked SO fabulous in their dresses, and they were bubbling with excitement. I really REALLY wanted to join in, but I just couldn't. The thought of what Diamonde and Gruella might do hung over me like a black cloud.

Diamonde was waiting in the marble corridor outside the grand ballroom. She scowled when she saw my friends, and pretended she was looking at a noticeboard. As Charlotte, Alice, Emily and the others floated through the ballroom door I hung back and went to meet her, my heart pitter-pattering in my chest.

Was I going to be brave? Or was I going to give in?

"Where's your tiara?" Diamonde demanded, and she held out a horrid tiara with bent feathers. "You can wear this one."

I took a deep breath. "No," I said. "I'm going to wear mine—"

"DIAMONDE!" Gruella rushed up to us. "Where have you BEEN?"

Diamonde's eyes flashed, and she snatched the tiara out of my hand.

"What are you DOING?" Gruella stared first at her sister, and then at my tiara. "WHAT'S THAT?"

Diamonde smirked. "I'm going to wear it this evening. Megan's lent it to me!"

"But what about ME?" Gruella's

face was bright red. "That means YOU'LL have a prettier tiara! That's not FAIR!" And she tried to snatch the tiara from Diamonde...but she couldn't.

It was so weird! Neither of them could let go of my beautiful tiara! They were totally and completely STUCK.

"Let GO!" yelled Gruella.

"I CAN'T!" shrieked Diamonde.

And as they stood there tugging

and pulling away, my friends came hurrying back to see where I was.

"Whatever's going on?" Charlotte asked.

"I'm STUCK!" Diamonde howled. "Take the horrid thing away!"

I stepped forward, and took hold of the tiara – and it was magic! All at once the twins were free! They gave one last screech, and dashed away wailing loudly.

"Goodness!" Sophia said. "Are you all right?"

I smiled at her. "I'm FINE," I said, and then I thought of something.

"Sophia," I said, "does it matter that I've never been to school before? Will I really be sent away from Silver Towers if the teachers find out?"

Sophia and the others looked at me in astonishment. "Of COURSE not," Alice said. "Whatever gave you that idea?"

"Oh – it was something Diamonde told me," I said. "It doesn't matter now."

"We won't let anyone send you away, EVER," Emily said, and she took my hand.

Charlotte nodded. "That's right! But hurry up and put your tiara on. We've got a Tiara Ball to go to!"

Chapter Six

What was the Tiara Ball like? It was MAGICAL!

We danced and danced all evening, and we whirled and we twirled in our beautiful dresses. Charlotte pointed out Queen Samantha Joy, our headteacher, and I couldn't help smiling because she was dancing the polka with a HUGE fairy.

"That's Fairy G, the head Fairy Godmother," Emily whispered. "She looks after us."

"Who's the pretty one?" I asked.

"That's Fairy Angora," Emily said. "Isn't her dress just glorious?"

I nodded, dazzled by the dress.

"She's not very good at magic, though," Emily chuckled.

But at that moment Fairy Angora waved her wand, and a cascade of twinkling silver stars flew up in

the air, then floated gently down, making our hair and our dresses sparkle in the most magical way.

I had to pinch myself to make sure I wasn't just having a miraculous dream. But it was all true...

And guess who won the silver rose for the most beautiful tiara

in the Tiara Parade?
  That's right! ME!

And that night, when I was snuggled up in my bed in Silver Rose Room, I couldn't help giving a MASSIVE sigh of happiness, because I had seven WONDERFUL new friends.

Who's the seventh?

Why, YOU of course!

Welcome to

The Tiara Club

Join the Rose Room princesses at the Princess Academy!

PRINCESS CHARLOTTE
AND THE BIRTHDAY BALL
ISBN 978 1 84362 863 7

PRINCESS KATIE
AND THE SILVER PONY
ISBN 978 1 84362 860 6

PRINCESS DAISY
AND THE DAZZLING DRAGON
ISBN 978 1 84362 864 4

PRINCESS ALICE
AND THE MAGICAL MIRROR
ISBN 978 1 84362 861 3

PRINCESS SOPHIA
AND THE SPARKLING SURPRISE
ISBN 978 1 84362 862 0

PRINCESS EMILY
AND THE BEAUTIFUL FAIRY
ISBN 978 1 84362 859 0

And join

More magical adventures with the Rose Room princesses!

PRINCESS CHARLOTTE
AND THE **ENCHANTED ROSE**
ISBN 978 1 84616 195 7

PRINCESS KATIE
AND THE **DANCING BROOM**
ISBN 978 1 84616 196 4

PRINCESS DAISY
AND THE **MAGICAL MERRY-GO-ROU**
ISBN 978 1 84616 197 1

PRINCESS ALICE
AND THE **CRYSTAL SLIPPER**
ISBN 978 1 84616 198 8

PRINCESS SOPHIA
AND THE **PRINCE'S PARTY**
ISBN 978 1 84616 199 5

PRINCESS EMILY
AND THE **WISHING STAR**
ISBN 978 1 84616 200 8

Look out for

The Tiara Club
at Ruby Mansions

Now make friends with the princesses from Poppy Room!

PRINCESS CHLOE AND THE
PRIMROSE PETTICOATS
ISBN 978 1 84616 290 9

PRINCESS JESSICA
AND THE BEST-FRIEND BRACELET
ISBN 978 1 84616 291 6

PRINCESS GEORGIA
AND THE SHIMMERING PEARL
ISBN 978 1 84616 292 3

PRINCESS OLIVIA
AND THE VELVET CLOAK
ISBN 978 1 84616 293 0

PRINCESS LAUREN
AND THE DIAMOND NECKLACE
ISBN 978 1 84616 294 7

PRINCESS AMY
AND THE GOLDEN COACH
ISBN 978 1 84616 295 4

And don't forget to join
the Tiara Club at Christmas time!

The Tiara Club

Win a Perfect Princess Tiara!

For your chance to win a tiara,
answer the following question:

*Who gave Princess Megan
her magical tiara?*

Send your answer and at least twenty words
on why you like the Tiara Club, plus
your name and your address, to:

The Tiara Club World Book Day Competition
Orchard Books
338 Euston Road
London NW1 3BH

Deadline for entries: 30 May 2007

Check out

website at:

www.tiaraclub.co.uk

You'll find Perfect Princess games and fun things to do, as well as news on the Tiara Club and all your favourite princesses!

This book has been specially written and published for World Book Day 2007.

World Book Day is a worldwide celebration of books and reading. This year marks the tenth anniversary of World Book Day in the United Kingdom and Ireland.

For further information please see
www.worldbookday.com

World Book Day is made possible by generous sponsorship from National Book Tokens, participating publishers, authors and booksellers. Booksellers who accept the £1 Book Token themselves fund the full cost of redeeming it.